Mice And The Moon

Three mice, thinking The Moon to be
made of cheese, go in search of a
ladder to climb up to it. But no matter
how high the ladders are they are never
long enough. Ultimately, it is being
faced with the choice between greed or
sharing the cheese that decides
whether the mice succeed or not.

T. William.

Tony Proof.

2017.

Late one night,
with The Moon so bright,
three hungry mice
looked up
and thought,

"It's round and it's yellow
with hues of blue.
It's obviously cheese
looking fresh and new."

"Let's find a ladder,"
said Mouse in the Middle.
So, off they went
hoping soon
to climb to The Moon.

They spied a ladder
of wood by a shed,
and that being said
Mouse in the Middle
put forward a riddle,

"It's just the right height
and obvious by sight
to see both ladder
and cheese will meet
when bottom and top
are plumb in the middle."

Not having a clue
of what was just said,
Mouse to the Left
and Mouse to the Right
took the ladder
into the night
with Mouse and his riddle
still in the middle.

Carrying the ladder
well at the back
Mouse to the Left
had a hunger attack,
and craved to devour
some Camembert Green
as well as some Cheddar
with a dollop of cream.

Then he wondered
whether or not
others would come
and scoff the lot,
and offered the thought
that just they three
should get to be
the only ones
to scoff the Brie.

The mice did then
agree to agree
to be as selfish
as a mouse could be.

They found a place in a field of grass
and held the ladder upright and fast.
Mouse in the Middle
scurried on up
and there on top
waved a paw high in the air,
then let out a cry,

"There ain't nothing here!
That lump of Cheddar and Brie
is out of reach
of this ladder and me!"

With whiskers abristle
and a frail red tail,
the mouse then squeaked
a subtle retort,
"This ladder, I feel,
is far too short!"
Then he called in a very loud manner,
"We're going to need a longer ladder!"

While walking through grass
and prickly sticks,
the mice came across
a chimney of bricks
with it's very own ladder
bolted and fixed.

So, using their tails
for wiggly tools
and prickly sticks
to pry the bricks,
they took the bolts
away from the wall
and took the ladder,
bolts and all.

While looking like cheese
floating with ease,
The Moon was a witness
to what it saw...

...three hungry mice
carrying a ladder,
with steps that numbered
more than before,

While confusing
and somewhat amusing
The Moon never uttered a word.

The three mice passed
others in grass,
and ever so quietly crept on by
so as not to share the cheese in the sky.

Then they raised the ladder upright
so Mouse in the Middle
could scurry on up
and there on top
with outstretched paw
he whispered clear,

"There ain't no cheese up here to scoff!
This ladder still ain't long enough!"

Then he whispered a little louder,

"We're going to need a
longer ladder!"

This should do it"
said Mouse in the Middle,
gazing at a clicketty-clack
railway track
that appeared to go
right to The Moon
The mice then took
the line unseen
when a light
it turned to green.

The Moon was a witness
to the sight of a train
come to a stop
at a light
of red
without
a sign
of a
line
ahead.

"We'll raise it here,"
said Mouse in the Middle,
carrying the brunt
of the ladder in front.

"What?" said Mouse at the Back
in a valley of green
where he couldn't be seen.

With a ladder, so long
he wished he had help.
His brothers and sister
would have been there
if he hadn't mentioned
not wanting to share.

Then he wondered how it could be
he had two brothers
while his sister had three.

Again they raised
the ladder on high
so Mouse in the Middle
could climb to the sky.

He scurried and hurried
where clouds were hollow
and nasty cats
dared never to follow.

He climbed so far
his tail was soon
above a star.
And there in air
ever so rare
he said quite clear,

"Oh fiddle-de-dee
and fiddle-de stuff!
This ladder's still not long enough!".

Then in the sky
he saw a sight
that gave his fur
a stand up fright.

It was two mice on ladders
the very same height.
From the East and the West
they were differently dressed
in attire that could at best
be described, for a mouse
with fur and a tail,
as entirely overdressed.

All were trying to reach
the very same cheese
still floating in silence,
still floating with ease.

"It's mine!
"It's mine!"
"It's mine!"

squealed the
mice in a
manner not nice,
not wanting to share
but ready to fight
with fist and fur.

Then came a voice from down below
from a wise old mouse
who seemed to know
there was nothing to share
since not a ladder
was anywhere near
the cheese in the air.

"Because of your greed
   you'll never succeed.
But co-operate and share
   and maybe you'll get
to the cheese up there.
   Use what's around
from the vines on the ground
   and tether together
three ladders as one."

The mice did then
agree to agree
to be as kind
as a mouse could be.

Hearing the news
of getting a share,
dozens of mice
did gather there.

With rolled up sleeves
they tethered together
the longest of ladders
with vines and leaves.

Each did fear the slightest sneeze
from sniffing and snuffing
would send the ladder
crashing to nothing.

Up and up it carefully rose,
held by micey
fingers and toes.

It rose and rose,
so gingerly rose.

Up and up...
Up and up

.untill!....

S....n.... a.....p!

A vine did break..
The ladder did shake.
and wibble and wobble
then slowly topple

"Ooooh!" and "Yaahg!" and "Nooooǃ"

the mice on top
were heard to go,

Then when totally out of control,
Mouse in the Middle put out a paw
as he'd done so often before.
But instead of air
he felt something there.

Was it a plate or was it a spoon?

.....No! It was The Moon!!!......

The ladder had finally reached The Moon!

Now
upon
The Moon

Mouse
in
the
Middle
remembered
his
promise
to
share
it with
all and
began
throwing   it down.

Down,

down,

The

Moon did

go

to

feed

the

mice

down

below.

Having had their fill
of Camembert cheese
and dollops of cream,
the three mice saw
a bright red star.

Was it Jupiter
or was it Mars?
Or was it a plum
that appealed
to their tum?

Mouse in the Middle
called once more
to all below
as he'd done before,

"It doesn't matter!
We're going to need
a longer ladder!"

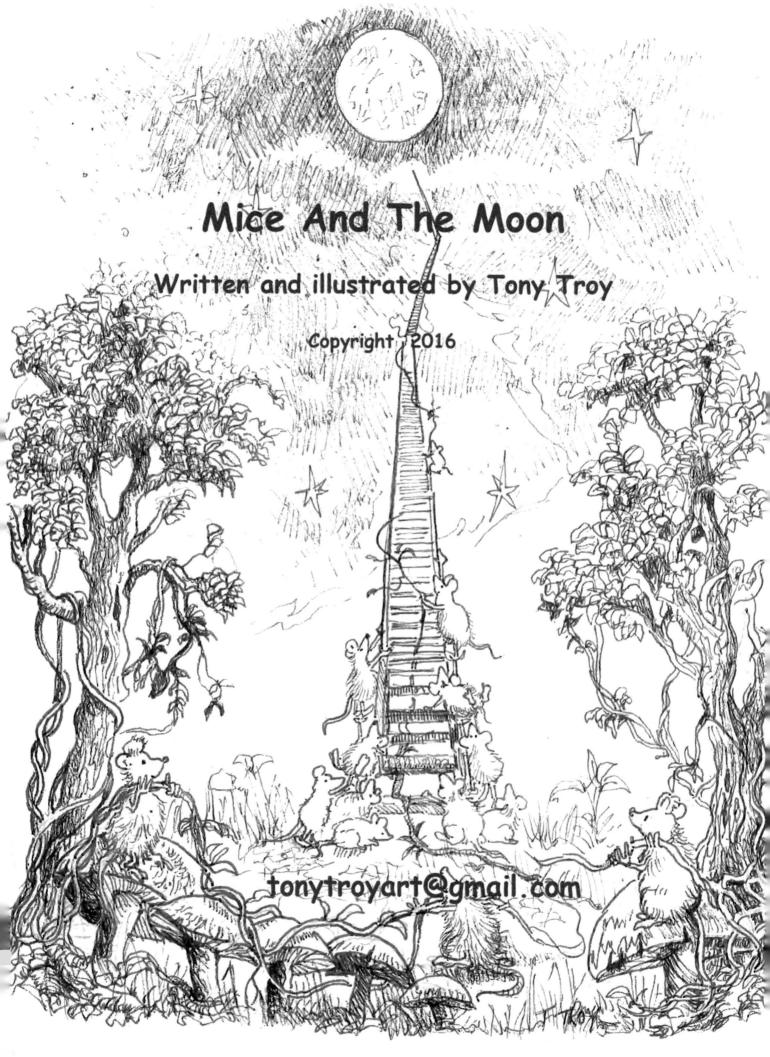

Mice And The Moon

Written and illustrated by Tony Troy

Copyright 2016

tonytroyart@gmail.com

Made in the USA
Middletown, DE
11 August 2017